W9-AYO-566

For Dieter, Clara, Angela and Lilian

Copyright © 1991 by Ruth Brown
All rights reserved.
CIP Data is available.
First published in the United States 1991 by
Dutton Children's Books,
a division of Penguin Books USA Inc.
Originally published in Great Britain by Andersen Press Limited,
20 Vauxhall Bridge Road, London SW1V 2SA
First American Edition   Printed in Verona, Italy, by Grafiche AZ
10 9 8 7 6 5 4 3 2
ISBN: 0-525-44635-4

The World That Jack Built

RUTH BROWN

FOREST HILL ELEMENTARY SCHOOL
WEST PALM BEACH, FL

DUTTON CHILDREN'S BOOKS   NEW YORK

This is the house that Jack built.

These are the trees that grow by the house that Jack built.

This is the stream that flows past the trees that grow
by the house that Jack built.

These are the meadows that border the stream,
that flows past the trees that grow by the house
that Jack built.

These are the woods that shelter the meadows,
that border the stream, that flows past the trees
that grow by the house that Jack built.

These are the hills that form the valley, that surrounds
the woods, that shelter the meadows, that border the stream,

that flows past the trees that grow by the house
that Jack built.

These are the hills that form the valley next to the one
that surrounds the woods, that shelter the meadows,

that border the stream, that flows past the trees that grow
by the house that Jack built.

And these are the woods that cover those hills,

and shelter the meadows,

that border the stream,

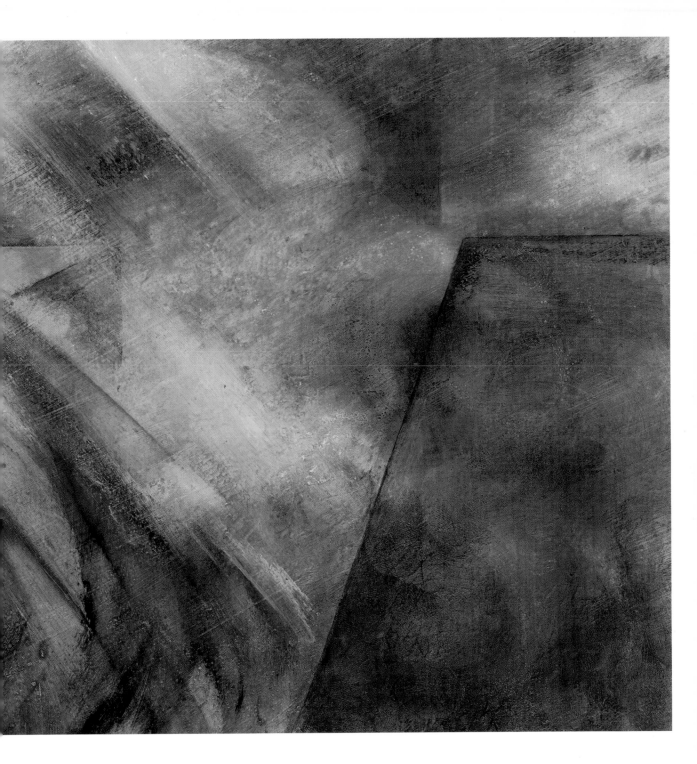

that flows past the place where the trees used to grow,

next to the factory that Jack built.